THE PASSOVER ZOO SEDER

The Passover Zoo Seder

S. Daniel Guttman • Illustrations by Phillip Ratner

PELICAN PUBLISHING COMPANY
Gretna 2011

To my mother, Sylvia, who would have enjoyed this.
To my Doda, Sarah Altman, who laughed at the least provocation.
To my Saba, Israel Galad, who led Seders as though he was a Formula One
*   racing driver and whose refrain was "Keep on Movin'."*
To my family, Marvie, Ian, and Justin: without them, a Seder would just be
*   another meal.*

—S.D.G.

The word "Pelican" and the depiction of a pelican are trademarks
of Pelican Publishing Company, Inc., and are registered in the
U.S. Patent and Trademark Office.

ISBN: 9781589809727

Printed in Singapore
Published by Pelican Publishing Company, Inc.
1000 Burmaster Street, Gretna, Louisiana 70053

Notes to Children: Past, Present, and Future

Many of us have been to Seders that seem like zoos, only the zoo animals are much better behaved. However, family, history, and religion keep us coming back to a place that is warm and familiar be it ever changing. Passover should be both fun and serious. This book belongs to the fun part.

How to Read This Book

The Passover Zoo Seder is meant to be read ALOUD to children of all ages with your own animal ululations and other sound effects added, as needed.

When to Read This Book and to Whom

Read it in the morning, at noon, or instead of a midnight snack. Read it to grandparents, children, grandchildren, parents, and selected strangers.

Read it before, during, and after the Seder. Read it in the bathtub, while brushing your teeth, before going to sleep, as you pretend you are sleeping, at the same time as jumping on a pogo stick, prior to sliding into second base, instead of eating your vegetables, simultaneously to saying a Bracha, subsequent to flying a kite, or as a good excuse for not doing your homework. But NEVER, EVER, NEVER read *The Passover Zoo Seder* when visiting the zoo. You might disturb the animals.

Anxious animals at the Great Zoo,
Fussed and wondered, "Whatever to do?"
With Passover near,
Queer sighs hit your ear.
Their Haggadahs were worn through and through.

Passover   פסח

Matzah   מצה

Maror   מרור

F ierce Fire Ants . . .
Danced a hot dance.
Fresh Fruit Flies. . .
Tossed ripe peach pies.
Unhappy Hawks . . .
Howled hoarse screeched squawks.
Normally mild, Connie Condor was sore.
But Lion was wild and let out a **Ma-Roar!**

Lion decided, as king of the beasts,
He was not going to miss the king of feasts.
So he growled and he scratched,
And soon he dispatched
His pawed Royal Orders
To the zoo's distant borders:
"If you fly, if you crawl, if you run or you swim,
Get up fast, floss your teeth, and rush, rush right to him."

The animals stormed through the bars and the cracks—
Cages broke, roofs collapsed, nests fell down, and hives lost wax.
They lined up around him, from the chimp to the boar,
And Lion applauded and let out a **Ma-Roar!**

Maroar

מרור

צ "You've all heard the news," he remarked with deep
   sorrow.
"We have no Haggadahs for Pesach tomorrow.
We'll just have to rely (as he picked up his scent)
On the world's greatest memory—Shai Elephant,
Who has always remembered a peanut he should
And has memorized almost the whole of Talmud.
Shai is not shy!
He has led many Seders. He'll teach you a part.
So line up, grab a pen, take a pad, and let's start."

ike thunder Shai rumbled to the top of the mound;
The animals grumbled while they gathered around.
Shai assigned them Seder parts—some were short,
  some were long.
Cousin Cockroach felt stomped on 'cause he got not
  one song.
Lola Llama was livid; Ian Iguana was green;
Jealous Justin J. Jaguar begged to sing song sixteen.
And Engineer Norman the Gnu said, "Nu-Nu!
I've urgent, more important projects to do."

"**E**nough griping, stop complaining, cut out kvetching!" roared Lion.
"Get to work; use your brains; practice hard; stop your cryin'."
So they scattered like fleas in a breeze, if you please.
And their hurricane shook all the leaves off the trees.

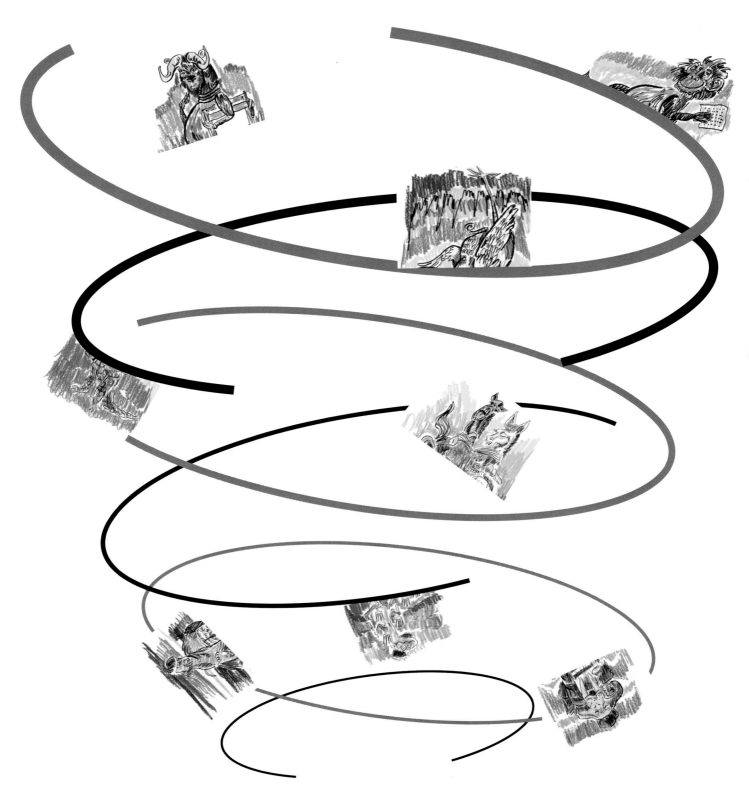

ד o get clean for the Seder, a bath they all took:
Doves in dust, moths in mud, rhinos rolled in gray gook.
Then they came and they came 'til you couldn't fit more,
And Lion approved and let out a **Ma-Roar!**

Lost Leopards leaped linens, queasy stomachs in knots,
'Til dogs sniffed their place cards, spotting leopards their spots.
Pithy Python in greeting her friends was no tease—
No fake smooching the air, her sincere snakish squeeze.
Antsy Anteater nibbled on some chocolates with his nose.
His rash is shaped like Moses from his allergies, I suppose.

Brother Bear found a plump porcupine to lean on as a pillow.
"Me be Burning Bush," bawled battered Bear. Now he's called
   "Weeping Willow."
The Charoset was chopped by Squirmy Worm with some dread.
He once fell in a blender, almost losing his head.

Carrot Tsimmes with honey was brought by Rude Rabbits;
They made such a big tsimmes, their worst of bad habits.
Seder's beautiful spread was set up by Stiff Storks.
Klutzy Centipede prayed he'd not drop fifty forks.

Pharoah-proud Peacocks paraded, the abject slaves of new fashion.
Whitefish were Gefilte—snacks Loony Loons craved with passion.
Marvelous Marmoset Marvie murmured Mom's *Hadleek Nair,*
She got too close to the candles, slightly singeing her hair.

Wally Walrus whined wine's Kiddush and wiped away wet tears,
And this was odd, because you know, he hadn't cried in years.
Laughing Harry Hyena, with his son and his pa,
Broke everyone up with "*Ha ha lach mah ahn Ya.*"

5o they started the Seder—"*Maaah Nishtanaaah,*" yelped young sheep, "*Hah-lye-laaaah hazeeeh*"—they could bleat in their sleep.
Eager animals answered with voices so furious.
Each species had their own chants; their praying was curious.

Passover פסח

Lolo Locust laser-focused on the Passover plot,
It plagued him that in Egypt, a hero he was not.
Velvel Virus from papyrus read the *Mowtzee* with a wheeze.
"So, so sorry," he said, sneezing, "I've contracted a disease."
Then the food was made ready; it looked and smelled nice.
Savta Ceil Sephardi (lucky yak) could only eat rice.

The salt-watered eggs of the hens were divine.
Most chickens were sad, but the foxes felt fine.
Though the termites liked matzah, the taste was so good,
Their gourmets would have added a sprinkling of wood.

The afikoman was stolen by Chief Bobby of a baboon tribe.
They could end Passover's meal—just peel him a banana bribe.
Bob surrendered it freely—the thief knew the score,
He fretted, drops were sweated—at Lion's **Ma-Roar!**

Matzah מַצָּה

Birkat Hamazon was mooed by harmonizing cows.
They refused to sit down 'til they had milked nine long bows.

Horsey and Donkey whinnied all of *Dah-yaynoo:*
"*Eeloo Neiiiiigh-tahn, Braaaay-tahn Lahnoo.* Thank you. Thank you."
"*Ehlee-yahoo Ha-Nahvee,*" buzzed Beaded Bea Bee.
"*Eh-hahd Meow Yoday-ah?*" queried Carl the Cool Cat.
"*Eh-hahd Aniiiiiii Yoday-ah,*" replied Righteous Ron Rat.
"*Diz-ahbin Ah-bah Tweet Tweet Zoo-zay,*"
Chirped Perky Parakeet, "And have a nice holiday."

ד his Zoo Seder was famous; it made all the headlines . . . "STARVING ANIMALS FULL NOW, BUT NONE STOOD IN BREADLINES."

Picky Vultures made sure that the table was clean;
They had big bones to pick, if you know what I mean.

וt was later than late, the crocodiles' curfews were broken.
Weary Wasps worried; Sleepy Skunks scurried, so few
 words were spoken.
Pushed to hurrying home, hippos broke down his door,
And the Seder concluded with Lion's **Ma-Roar!**

Maroar מרור

Passover Zoology

Afikoman: A piece of matzah that is hidden by the Seder leader to be brought out later to finish the meal. This piece of matzah is stolen when the leader isn't looking and ransomed later by the child-thieves for anything from a gold watch to another piece of matzah, depending on how anxious everyone is to finish the meal. Smart children keep around a piece of matzah from last year as a decoy.

Birkat Hamazon: Blessing at the end of the meal (see Mowtzee and Bracha). A fine symmetry when combined with Mowtzee. Must be recited—with or without heartburn.

Bracha: A blessing. Way beyond "God bless you" for a sneeze. There is a blessing for everything, real and imaginary, and this one reminds us to be grateful. A comeuppance for ingrates.

Charoset: Symbolizes the mortar used by the Israelite slaves in building the pyramids—but tastes better and is not recommended for repaving driveways. It is typically manufactured with nuts, apples, and wine.

"Dah-yaynoo . . . Lahnoo": A listing of all the things we have to be thankful for, each of which alone would be sufficient, includes the Sabbath, the Torah, escape from Egypt, etc. However, it does not include central air-conditioning, microwaves, and pooper scoopers.

"Diz-ahbin . . . Zoo-zay": "Chad Gadya" is an Aramaic chant or cumulative tale along the lines of "This is the house that Jack built." A kid (i.e., young goat) is eaten by a cat, which is bitten by a dog, which is beaten by a stick, etc. Finally, the "Holy one, blessed be He" slays the Angel of Death. Do not attempt this at home. With its violent theme, the song should be labeled PG-13, but it is a children's favorite. The Seder is over and the stampede home begins.

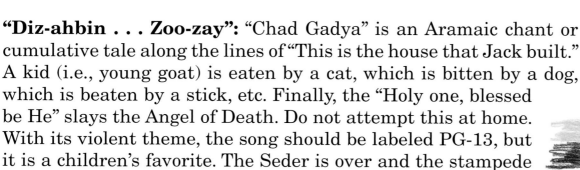

"Eh-hahd Meow Yoday-ah": The first of a total of thirteen themes and concepts central to Judaism. Maimonides had thirteen basic tenets of belief. So thirteen, which is not an unlucky number in Judaism, is a prime number on several levels. Who knows the first theme?

Gefilte: Literally means "filled" and is a precursor to Hamburger Helper—created in the old country but used for fish. To make, grind fish, add extending ingredients, bake, and don't forget the horseradish garnish. It tastes better than it sounds.

Haggadah: Recitation of the story of Passover. In some families, it seems to take the original forty years of desert wandering; in others, it's only forty seconds. The Haggadah includes biblical stories, homilies, exegeses, and songs. In short, there is something for everyone.

Ha ha lach mah ahn Ya: Literally means "This bread of affliction" (referring to matzah). The expression possibly originated by Israelites with poor digestion.

Hadleek Nair: The lighting of the candles by the matriarch, which ushers in every Sabbath and holiday. Typically, not enough light is shed to illuminate solutions to family squabbles.

Kiddush: Blessing over the wine. Among all Jewish holidays, four consumed cups are uniquely mandated at a Passover Seder. Fortunately, there is no quiz at the end, and a designated driver is not generally required.

Kvetching: Yiddish for complaining about your complaints, as in " I can't possibly be well because I am feeling too good, so something must be wrong with me because this isn't normal, Doctor." All hypochondriacs kvetch by definition, but not all kvetchers are hypochondriacs. They may have other specialties. The only hope for cure is rehab in the Kvetch Clinic.

"Maaah Nishtanaah . . . Hah-lye-laaaah hazeeh": "Why is this night different from all other nights?" This is the first of the four questions, which the youngest participant of the Seder traditionally asks. Sometimes the questioners are forty years old and ask the same questions each year. Is that annoying or what? The fifth traditional question—prompted by growling stomachs—is, "Can we eat already?"

Ma-Roar: A "plague" on words. Hebrew for the bitter herb, often horseradish, this phrase reminds us that as bad as things are now, they could be worse. An antidote for the optimist.

Matzah: The original fast food, a cracker on steroids. The Israelites rushed out of Egypt without their automatic breadmakers. Given the hot pursuit by the Egyptians, pumpernickel with raisins was out of the question, so the Israelites only had enough time to produce unleavened flat bread, which, in turn, thousands of years later spawned the cream cheese industry.

Mowtzee: Blessing over bread or matzah (see Bracha). "Blessed art thou Oh Lord our God, King of the Universe, who bringest forth bread from the earth." For day old bread, use the past tense.

Nu-Nu: Yiddish for "Well," "So what," "Keep on moving," "What's on your mind?" A pithy, all-purpose exclamation popularized by Nathan Detroit in *Guys and Dolls,* as in "So, Nu? Sue me."

Pesach: Hebrew for Passover. God "passed over" the houses of the Israelites during the last of the ten plagues—the slaying of the firstborn. They left a night light on for the Angel of Death.

Salt-watered eggs: The salt-water symbolizes the Israelites' tears over being slaves in Egypt. It also reminds us how we slightly more recently cried when we grated horseradish and cut onions for the Seder.

Seder: Literally means a systematic or orderly event and refers to the Passover meal and its accompanying Haggadah recitation. In many homes, a Seder is an oxymoron.

Talmud: A tour de force of rabbinical discourse. Got an opinion? You can probably find it in the Talmud. Starting with the Torah or Five Books of Moses, there are commentaries on . . . you get the idea.

IN THIS ZOO YOU MAY PLAY WITH THE ANIMALS!

HOW TO GET TONGUE-TIED

Moses was known to have a speech impediment, so he might have had a hard time with the tongue twisters sprinkled throughout our story. Here are a couple of samples to try out on your older or younger siblings. Say "Hoarse screeched-squawks" and "Pithy Python" five times fast.

WARNING: Stay far enough away so you don't get a spray. See if you can find other jawbreakers.

PASSOVER ZOO SEDER WORD SAFARI

```
R E Z E E U Q S H S I K A N S F O O R M E
A N G S S T N A E R I F E C R E I F N I D
E G Q H H T U R O D N O C E I N N O C S S
B I Q A C F S H N C O O K W C B I O L K E
R N H I A N S E I G R E L L A L U F W W G
E E A E M C I D N V P M P T R S R A N A A
H E D L O H C E R U E I H E I E U C E H C
T R A E T O W Q Z A P S T N S Q G S C Y Q
O N G P S C Q E Q E P A C H S A O U N P I
R O G H Y O I Y A V E O F D Y N C P A P A
B R A A S L O N Y T C R E D M P R H D A N
D M H N A A U Z N K U H B L Y I Y G T H I
I A A T E T Y A R I C S E A T U R T O N G
R N M U U E Y O T E P H E N N S V S H U U
A T A B Q S A F E B V A U I A I O Y N O A
X H L B T C L R A S H O N H P C S L S S N
I E L N H I C S M O S E S C T H I A C B A
N G A J E S G O D U N I L S H D C R E Q L
T N L S L S J U S T I N J J A G U A R L J
W U O V O P L U M P P O R C U P I N E U F
T A L M U D X X U V G F O Q K X X E H R P H
```

ALLERGIES, ANTSYANTEATER, BATH, BROTHERBEAR, CAGES, CHOCOLATES, CONNIECONDOR, COUSINCOCKROACH, DOGS, ENGINEERNORMANTHEGNU, FIERCEFIREANTS, FLEASINABREEZE, FRESHFRUITFLIES, HAGGADAH, HIVES, HOTDANCE, HURRICANE, IANIGUANA, JUSTINJJAGUAR, LION, LOLALLAMA, LOSTLEOPARDS, MOSES, NESTS, NOSE, PASSOVERZOOSEDER, PEACHPIES, PEANUT, PESACH, PITHYPYTHON, PLUMPPORCUPINE, QUEASYSTOMACHS, RASH, ROOFS, SCREECHEDSQUAWKS, SHAIELEPHANT, SNAKISHSQUEEZE, TALMUD, UNHAPPYHAWKS

IT'S PASSOVER—NOT A CROSS WORD!

ACROSS
3 Chief _____ the Baboon
7 Passover in Hebrew
11 He sat on a Porcupine
12 They did a hot dance
14 Not nice Rabbits can be this
15 _____ of the Beasts
16 No animal stood on these
21 Bee's first name
22 He lead many Seders
26 They asked the four questions
28 Locust wasn't one of these
29 Who knows one? He asked
30 Lion wouldn't _____ this feast
31 They took a bath to get this
32 Harry Hyena brought his son and him
33 What Shai Memorized
37 Afikoman Bribe
38 Python didn't smooch this
40 Rhino rolled in this
41 Cockroach got not _____ song
42 Caused Anteater to scratch
44 _____ Watered Eggs
47 Strange, for Walrus
49 You fly, crawl, run or this
53 He should avoid chocolate
55 This Seder made these in the Papers
56 Lions' sorrow ran

57 You crawl, run, swim or this

DOWN
1 Eliahoo Hanavi, she buzzed
2 Justin J. was Jealous
3 He stole the Afikoman
4 Get to work, use your _____
5 _____ Iguana
6 _____ J. Jaguar
8 Laughing Harry
9 You fly, run, swim or this
10 A hero he was not
12 Anteater suffered from these

13 They sniffed place cards
16 What Vultures picked
17 He wasn't shy
18 Horsey's Buddy
19 Ian _____ was green
20 Pharoah Land
23 This shook all the leaves
24 Anteater's enemy
25 He might drop

silverware
27 Flies tossed ripe ones
34 What Bobby stole
35 Lion's Refrain
36 They bathed in dust
39 Unusual for Walrus (sing.)
43 Donkeys' best friend
45 _____ Anteater
46 Walrus wiped away

these
48 What Bobby Baboon sweated
50 Since Lion wasn't tame he was
51 What Shai wasn't
52 Queer sighs hit this
54 Put these in salt-water (sing.)

For solutions to *The Passover Zoo Seder* puzzles or to contact the author, please visit Pelican's Web site at www.pelicanpub.com.